Daniel Goes Out for Dinner

adapted by Maggie Testa

based on the screenplay "A Night Out at the Restaurant"

written by Becky Friedman

poses and layouts by Jason Fruchter

Ready-to-Read

Simon Spotlight

New York   London   Toronto   Sydney   New Delhi

SIMON SPOTLIGHT
An imprint of Simon & Schuster Children's Publishing Division
1230 Avenue of the Americas, New York, New York 10020
This Simon Spotlight edition January 2015
© 2015 The Fred Rogers Company. All rights reserved.
All rights reserved, including the right of reproduction in whole or in part in any form.
SIMON SPOTLIGHT, READY-TO-READ, and colophon are registered trademarks of Simon & Schuster, Inc.
For information about special discounts for bulk purchases, please contact Simon & Schuster Special Sales at
1-866-506-1949 or business@simonandschuster.com.
Manufactured in the United States of America 0815 LAK
4 6 8 10 9 7 5 3
ISBN 978-1-4814-2872-9 (hc)
ISBN 978-1-4814-2871-2 (pbk)
ISBN 978-1-4814-2873-6 (eBook)

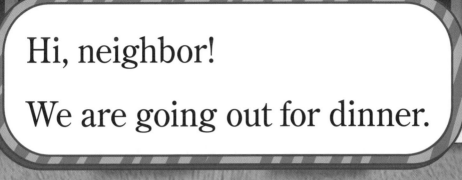

Hi, neighbor!

We are going out for dinner.

What food do you think looks yummy?

Yum!

Now we have to wait for our food to be cooked.

It is very, very

hard to wait.

"When you wait,
you can play, sing,
or imagine anything."

"We can play 'what is missing,'" says Katerina.

Look at the things
on the table.

Katerina hides

one of the things.

What is missing?

The salt was missing!

What should we do
while we wait?

When you wait,
you can play, sing,
or imagine anything.

We can imagine that the things on the table can play with us!

I am glad I waited
for my food.

It is so yummy!

I can play, sing,
or imagine anything
to make waiting easier.